MONSTERS

A **Strange Science** BOOK

SYLVIA FUNSTON

Illustrations by JOE WEISSMANN

Owl Books are published by Greey de Pencier Books Inc.
51 Front Street East, Suite 200, Toronto, Ontario M5E 1B3

The Owl colophon is a trademark of Owl Children's Trust Inc.
Greey de Pencier Books Inc. is a licensed user of trademarks of Owl Children's Trust Inc.

Distributed in the United States by Firefly Books (U.S.) Inc.
230 Fifth Avenue, Suite 1607, New York, NY 10001

We acknowledge the financial support of the Canada Council for the Arts, the Ontario Arts Council, and the Government of Canada through the Book Publishing Industry Development Program (BPIDP) for our publishing activities.

Dedication
To Susan and John, the kind of friends any monster would die for.

Cataloguing in Publication Data
Funston, Sylvia
        Monsters

"A Strange science book".
Includes index.
ISBN 1-894379-17-9 (bound)   ISBN 1-894379-18-7 (pbk.)

1. Monsters — Juvenile literature.   I. Weissman, Joe, 1947– .   II. Title.

GR825.F86   2001   j001.944   C00-932404-6

Design & art direction: Word & Image Design Studio Inc.
Illustrations: Joe Weissmann
Editor: Kat Motosune
Photo coordinator: Taryn Nirenberg

Photo Credits
Pages 4 and 22: Kent, Keith/Peter Arnold, Inc.; 7 (left): Coleman, Loren/Fortean Picture Library; 7 (right): Haneda, Dick; 8 and 9: Dahinden, René; 10 (main): Shiels, Anthony/Fortean Picture Library; 10 (inset): Hepburn, Austin/Fortean Picture Library; 24: Richardson, G.R./Robert Harding Picture Library; 29: G.R. Dick Roberts Photo Library; 30: Aarsleff, Klaus/Fortean Picture Library; 31: Seitre, Roland/Peter Arnold, Inc.; 32: CDC/LL/Peter Arnold, Inc.; 34 (main): Scharf, David/Peter Arnold, Inc.; 34 (inset): Kage, Manfred/Peter Arnold, Inc.; 35: Syred, Andrew/Science Photo Library; 36: Bannister, Anthony/NHPA

Printed in Hong Kong

A   B   C   D   E   F

Contents

Monster THRILLS

A world without monsters? How boring! Nothing matches the chills and thrills of feeling that something awful is lurking in the dark, while knowing you're safe snuggled under the bedclothes.

If people hadn't already created really worthwhile monsters, such as dragons, sea monsters and vampires, we'd have to invent them all over again. By now you're probably wondering if this book is going to spoil the fun and tell you that monsters don't exist outside our heads. Sorry, you're not going to escape that easily. The fact is everyone, at some time, comes across a real monster or two.

So what makes a monster? Is it their size, what they do or how they look? There's no strict rule about monsters. They come in all shapes and sizes. They can be funny, pitiful or scary. Some aren't too bright. They can be animals, humans, part animal-part human, vegetable, even mineral (like monster asteroids using Earth for target practice). And most look nothing like us. Big, scary, stupid, mixed-up and strange-looking—that just about sums up most monsters.

One important thing to remember is that what's a monster to you might not be a monster to someone else. (Someone, somewhere, might actually think your brother or sister is great.) Exploring monsters is a good way of finding out about ourselves.

**BEWARE OF TOXIC BREATH!
READ AT ARM'S LENGTH.**

Dragons and Griffins

Some monsters are celebrated in legends around the world. Many were invented to give heroes something scary to battle, to show the rest of us how to behave in tough situations. European dragons (see left) are huge, spiky lizards with wings and fiery breath, while the Mexican god Quetzalcoatl is a winged and feathered serpent. In India, dragons (called nagas) are magical creatures with human heads and the bodies of snakes. Asian dragons are miraculous animals with beards, scales, antlers, a horse's mane, tiger's paws and eagle's claws. They are revered for being good and wise, and medicines including dragon parts supposedly have great healing powers.

It's possible that people believed in dragons because of real animals. The Chinese name for a dinosaur is "kong long," which means "terrible dragon." The great dino extinction happened 65 million years ago, long before humans appeared. But early humans could have found dinosaur bones and let their imaginations do the rest.

For instance, ferocious monsters named griffins with the heads of eagles and the bodies of lions were first recorded 9000 years ago. Some think they were based on fossils of Protoceratops—a small dinosaur with an eagle-like skull and lion-like feet. Others think the griffin sprang from early people's memories of a huge prehistoric bird, called Titanis. Blessed with the speed of *T-rex* and a beak that could pierce body armor, Titanis must have been one totally terrifying bird.

Hard-boiled Eggs

According to legend, griffins (see right)—part eagle and part lion—laid eggs as hard as stone. This ancient belief might be explained if people who came across Protoceratops fossils thousands of years ago also found its fossilized eggs.

Bulls, Lions and What?

The Ishtar Gate in the ancient city of Babylon is covered with images of bulls, lions and this dragon-like creature. Could it be the *amphisbaena*, an African dragon with two heads—one in front and one at the end of its tail? Or is it the mysterious Mokele-mbembe (see page 10), which some think might be a sauropod dinosaur still living in the swamps of west Africa?

Here Be Dragons

Maps made by sailors long ago had the note "Here Be Dragons" through what is now Malaysia and Indonesia, home of the Komodo dragon (photo above). These fearsome lizards still exist today, and can grow to be as long as a car. They have huge, curved and serrated teeth, and their bite is toxic. Their yellow, forked tongues flick in and out of their mouths, looking like a flame.

Fabulous
BEASTS

The Grisly Folk Live?

"The Almastys are like people—except that they are covered with hair—they do not know how to speak; they only mumble or bellow. They are not afraid of people, only of dogs." That is how a villager from the Caucasus Mountains in central Asia described the wild people he saw in his youth. Some scientists think that if Almas are real, they might have descended from the Neanderthals—famous author H.G. Wells called them "the grisly folk." Neanderthals disappeared after modern humans moved into Europe. Could they have married into the human tribe, or maybe retreated to remote mountainous areas to avoid human contact?

This famous image is from an amateur film taken in 1967 by Roger Patterson and Robert Gimlin in northern California. The film and the plaster cast of one of the creature's huge footprints (see photo on opposite page, with ruler and man's foot for size) are cited by many people as proof that Bigfoot exists.

Hairy Monsters

The monsters we imagine and create in our minds are usually overpoweringly big and mean. So if we created Bigfoot—a.k.a. Sasquatch—why did we make it no taller than a basketball player and so shy we're lucky to catch even a glimpse of it? Not exactly in the same league as King Kong, is it? There's something that rings true about a not-so-big, extremely shy Bigfoot. Could it really exist?

Some people think Bigfoot might be a new type of ape we never knew existed. Others think it might be a living fossil, directly descended from an apelike creature known as Gigantopithecus that became extinct 300,000 years ago. It's a puzzle. People have made casts of huge footprints, taken photographs—even made a home movie of Bigfoot. But this evidence can all be the product of known natural phenomena; the footprints could be made by bears, or enlarged by snow melting—or of hoaxes—the film could be of a person in a hairy suit. No one knows what Bigfoot is or whether it really exists. But believing that there's something wild and hairy (besides bears and hikers) living in North America's west coast mountains might give you a nice little scare—so go on and believe.

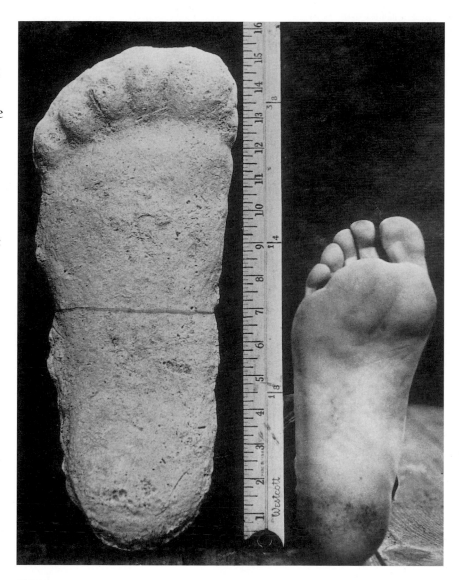

That There Thing

The Yeti is the Bigfoot of the Himalayas. Tibetan Sherpas called the *Yeti metoh kanqmi*—"abominable snowman." We call it Yeti, which means "that there thing." It's been seen often (no trees to hide behind) and people have photographed its footprints. However, the edges of prints in snow melt and then refreeze, so this evidence isn't too reliable. And the effect that high altitude climbing can have on the brain was demonstrated in the 1980s when an Englishman returned from the Himalayas with photographs of a Yeti. He claimed that it stood still for so long it might have been imitating a rock. A later expedition showed the Yeti wasn't imitating a rock—it was a rock.

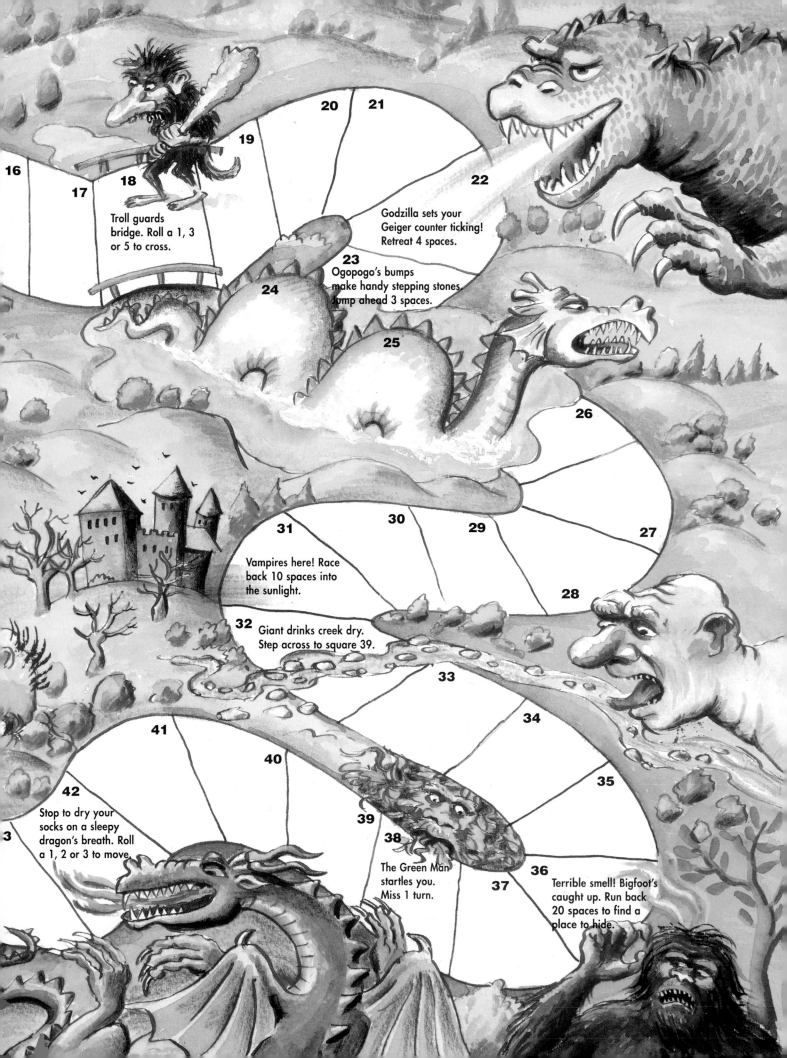

16

17

18

19

20 21

22

Troll guards bridge. Roll a 1, 3 or 5 to cross.

Godzilla sets your Geiger counter ticking! Retreat 4 spaces.

23 Ogopogo's bumps make handy stepping stones. Jump ahead 3 spaces.

24

25

26

31

30

29

27

28

Vampires here! Race back 10 spaces into the sunlight.

32 Giant drinks creek dry. Step across to square 39.

33

34

35

41

40

42

39

38

3

Stop to dry your socks on a sleepy dragon's breath. Roll a 1, 2 or 3 to move.

The Green Man startles you. Miss 1 turn.

36

37

Terrible smell! Bigfoot's caught up. Run back 20 spaces to find a place to hide.

HOW
to Make a Monster

Zap It

Nights were cold and wet in the summer of 1816 in Geneva. During a contest to see who could write the scariest story, Mary Shelley heard her husband Percy and another poet, Lord Byron, discussing the experiments of a Dr. Erasmus Darwin. Darwin sent an electrical current through a piece of spaghetti and, when it moved, claimed he had given it life! Around the same time, Luigi Galvani argued that electricity was the life force, and tried to revive dead animals with it. His nephew even applied electricity to a human corpse. Mary, who was the only one who actually finished writing her scary story, wrote about a young medical doctor who creates a monster by joining parts of dead bodies and re-animating them with electricity. You've probably heard the name of the doctor in Mary Shelley's story—Victor Frankenstein.

Nuke It

The movie monster Godzilla owes his monster breath problem to a large dose of radioactivity—he can fry objects up to 150 metres (500 feet) away! In real life, of course, massive doses of radioactivity are lethal. When a reactor at the Chernobyl nuclear power station in Russia exploded in 1986, large amounts of radiation escaped, causing devastation and death. But here's the odd thing—mice and voles seem to be thriving on Chernobyl's radioactive materials. What's scary is that while they look normal, their genes are rapidly mutating. Could radioactive mutant rodents be breeding near Chernobyl? Scientists are watching.

Dream It

Many cultures have stories of a monster that crushes you while you sleep. In Newfoundland the nightmare monster is known as the Old Hag. People who've met her say they were lying in bed, relaxed but awake, when suddenly they couldn't move because she was sitting on their chest, choking them. The Old Hag got a lot of bad press until researchers discovered that she's blameless. When we sleep, our brain sends out signals that paralyze our muscles, so we don't hurt ourselves acting out our dreams. A very tired brain might get confused and freeze our muscles while we're still awake. So we can't move, and the sensation is like being pinned to the bed by a monster.

By Accident

Want to see a real Cyclops? You'll need a microscope. There is a one-eyed water flea called Cyclops (see right), but it's too tiny to give Polyphemus a run for his money. The water flea naturally has only one eye, but accidents also happen in nature. Sometimes lambs are born with only a single eye. Why? Before the lamb is born, the front part of its brain fails to divide normally and produce two eyes. The problem can be caused by a fault in a gene that tells cells how they should develop. And by the 1960s scientists knew that outbreaks of "cyclopia" in lambs can also be caused by poisons in corn lily plants that their mothers eat while they are pregnant.

When the World Gets
SCARY

This lightning storm in Wisconsin is scary, even if people no longer think a monster is the cause of it.

WARNING! MONSTERS IN BAD MOODS HERE!

Monstrous Weather

Long before people discovered the magic of science, they hadn't a clue how the world worked. So they created monsters to explain things like terrible storms, earthquakes and disease. Thinking they knew how or why frightening things happened made people feel more in control of their lives.

According to Blackfoot legend, the mighty Thunderbird causes thunderstorms. This great spirit of the storm wraps himself in dark clouds. Thunder rolls from his flapping wings and lightning strikes from his eyes. Wherever he flies, rain falls. Today we still cancel our picnic plans if we see a thundercloud forming. Knowing it's a fast rising column of warm air that's building up a huge electric charge as water droplets jostle around inside it makes it scary, even if it isn't Thunderbird's fault. Eventually some of the electricity will discharge and— zap!— lightning will sear a pathway through the air as it leaps to the ground. During the lightning flash electricity will flow back and forth along this pathway at least twice, sometimes more, heating up the air and making it expand noisily. The faster the air expands, the louder it will rumble.

There once lived a great-horned monster named Gong-Gong. He tore such a hole in the side of Mt. Buzhou that he triggered a disastrous flood. When Gong-Gong wasn't impaling mountains, he was ripping holes in the sky. At least, that's what the ancient Chinese thought was happening when they tried to explain why the weather and the sky were so changeable.

Do Mountains Get Indigestion?

Following the volcanic eruption of Japan's Mount Usu in the year 2000, cracks big enough to swallow houses opened up in the earth around its base. Is it any wonder that when ancient Slavonic people came across a similar kind of crack in the earth's surface, they thought they were looking into the gaping mouth of a people-gobbling witch? They tell stories of Baba-Yaga, a powerful witch who lives in a hut that travels on huge chicken's legs, which would be pretty useful when the earth starts to crack.

THUNDERBIRD'S ON ITS WAY

You can tell how far away lightning is by counting the seconds between the flash and the rumble of thunder, then dividing by three. If you count six seconds, the lightning is 2 km (1.2 miles) away. If there's a simultaneous flash and loud bang, watch out! The lightning's right above you.

23

When the World Gets SCARY

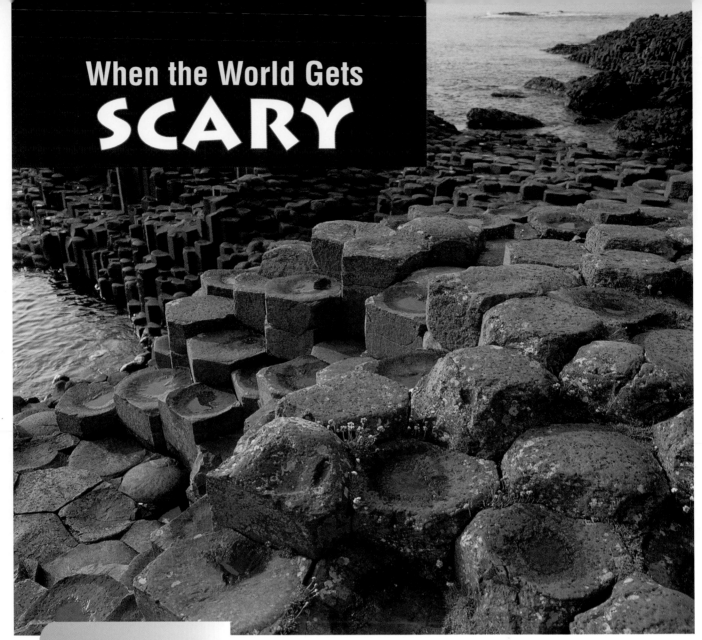

The Giant's Causeway, in Northern Ireland, is made up of such huge and perfect six-sided rock columns that people thought a monster must have made it. It gets its name from the legend that the giant Finn Mac Cool built it.

LOOK OUT! GIANT ROAD WORK AHEAD.

Rock Monsters

About 60 million years ago, volcanoes along the western edge of the British Isles spewed out very hot, fast-flowing basalt lava. Some flowed into the sea, cooling rapidly and shrinking. As shrinking basalt crystallizes, it cracks in a regular six-sided hexagon pattern—the same one that bees use to build their honeycomb. The pattern allows the largest number of rock columns (or honey cells) to be packed together in a given space—looking as if they've been carefully arranged by hand.

It would take a very large hand to arrange all the basalt columns that form the Giant's Causeway on the north coast of Northern Ireland. Legend has it that the giant Finn Mac Cool built this sturdy road across the sea to the Scottish island of Staffa so he could visit his rival, the giant Finn Gal.

Finn Mac Cool was so tired when he finished the road that he crawled home for a nap. While he was snoring up a storm, Finn Gal walked the road to Ireland. When Mrs. Mac Cool slyly told him that the sleeping giant was her baby son, Finn Gal imagined how big the huge baby's father might be. Scared, he ran back to Staffa, ripping up the road as he went. That's why all that's left of the Giant's Causeway today are its two ends—one on the beach near Ballycastle and the other on the island of Staffa.

Stone Warriors

The Iroquois nations believed that there once lived a race of evil stone giants known as Chenoo. They hurled boulders around as if they were pebbles, used trees as clubs, and they decided that humans must die. The Iroquois called upon the god of the west wind for help. He swooped down with such force that he blew the Chenoo over the edge of a cliff. Their broken stone bodies can still be seen to this day, piled up at the base of the cliff.

Rock and Troll

You probably know trolls as tiny dolls with bright colored hair, or as unpleasant creatures that live under bridges and bother innocent travellers. But in old Scandinavian tales, trolls are giant, monstrous beings that hate humans and haunt the woods at night, scaring people half to death. Like vampires, these early trolls are doomed to live by moonlight. If exposed to sunlight they turn to stone. What a wonderfully creepy way to explain strange outcrops of hard rock that haven't weathered as fast as the softer rocks surrounding them.

Here Be Sea MONSTERS

Seven Sea Stories

Before the days of power-driven, steel-hulled ships, and modern maps and satellites to tell exactly where you are, sailing was hazardous. Many a ship disappeared without trace. Is it any wonder that sailors created sea monsters?

The giant kraken was the mightiest sea monster of all. When it surfaced, the water boiled and ships ran aground on its massive back. When it submerged, it created a whirlpool that sucked in ships. A modern sailor would say that boiling water is a sign of dangerous rip tides and currents, and that ships run aground on shallow, sandy shoals or submerged reefs. Whirlpools form naturally in narrow channels where water meets from two different directions.

Stormin' Stormalong

American folk hero Alfred Bulltop Stormalong was sailing where waters between Norway and Denmark meet the North Sea, when the surface started to boil. As the kraken broke the surface, Stormalong harpooned it. Then he held tight to the harpoon rope as the kraken submerged, opening a whirlpool. As the whirlpool grew larger, Stormalong eased out the rope and his ship raced around its rim. When he released the rope, the spinning force of the whirlpool flung the ship out of danger.

Two Sea Monsters for the Price of One

The same Odysseus who escaped the Cyclops had to sail through a narrow strait guarded by two monsters. The first, six-headed Scylla, lived in a cave high on the rocky cliffs. The second, Charybdis, was a whirlpool monster that ate whole ships. Odysseus got his ship through the strait, but only after Scylla had claimed six of his crew.

What Old Ears You've Got

Merpeople, like the Mariner in the movie *Waterworld*, are part-humans who breathe underwater through gills. It's been 300 million years since our amphibian ancestors had gills, but our genes might have a memory of them. If we could locate it, could we grow them? After all, scientists can now tap into gene memories and create mutant mice with the hearing system they had 200 millions years ago.

I Wanna Hold Your (Eight) Hands

According to the owner of a company that runs scuba cruises off British Columbia's Gulf Islands, the giant Pacific octopus can be coaxed to hold your hand.

Whale of a Tale

From the whale that swallowed Jonah in the Bible, to the famous great white Moby Dick, to Willy (who needed to be freed), whales are intimidating by their huge size. But the biggest whales eat only plankton, little tiny sea creatures. Because humans have hunted whales until they are endangered, whales might have their own monster stories about us!

Scary Skerries

One of the world's most dangerous whirlpools is found at the northeastern tip of Scotland, where water from the Atlantic Ocean meets water from the North Sea. The results are rip tides, areas of shallow water and a gigantic whirlpool known as the Skerries, which has "eaten" many ships over the centuries.

The Kraken Lives

The "kraken" on this page fits everyone's idea of a monster—it's big enough to battle sperm whales and has even been known to attack ships. But this giant squid is real!

At the center of the ring formed by its eight arms and two longer tentacles sits a hard beak. Powerful mouth muscles turn and protrude this snapping beak so it doesn't miss a mouthful. This monster has teeth everywhere! Even its tongue is lined with backward-facing teeth, known as radula, which help grind up food and move it down the beast's gullet.

Two long tentacles end in clublike ends. It's easy to see how, from a distance, the broad end of a tentacle breaking the surface might look like the head of a sea serpent.

Squid suckers sit on short stalks, move independently of each other and are armed with a ring of teeth that grab hold of slippery prey. Round scars are often found on the skin of sperm whales.

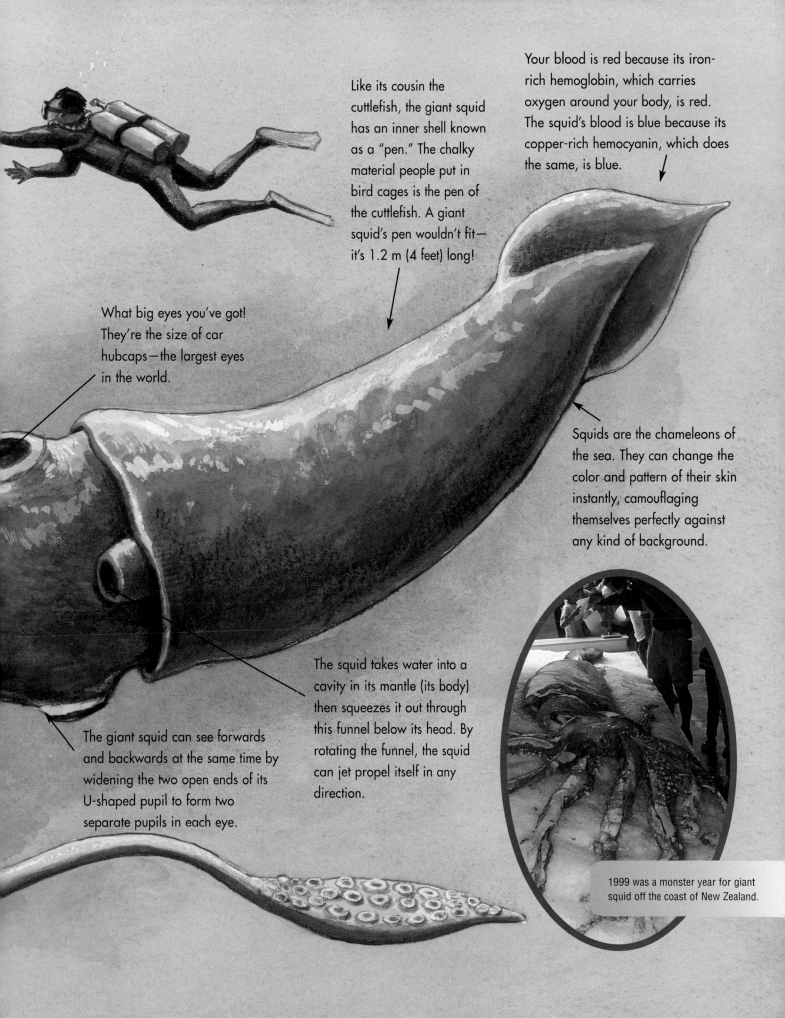

Like its cousin the cuttlefish, the giant squid has an inner shell known as a "pen." The chalky material people put in bird cages is the pen of the cuttlefish. A giant squid's pen wouldn't fit— it's 1.2 m (4 feet) long!

Your blood is red because its iron-rich hemoglobin, which carries oxygen around your body, is red. The squid's blood is blue because its copper-rich hemocyanin, which does the same, is blue.

What big eyes you've got! They're the size of car hubcaps—the largest eyes in the world.

Squids are the chameleons of the sea. They can change the color and pattern of their skin instantly, camouflaging themselves perfectly against any kind of background.

The giant squid can see forwards and backwards at the same time by widening the two open ends of its U-shaped pupil to form two separate pupils in each eye.

The squid takes water into a cavity in its mantle (its body) then squeezes it out through this funnel below its head. By rotating the funnel, the squid can jet propel itself in any direction.

1999 was a monster year for giant squid off the coast of New Zealand.

It's in Your BLOOD

NOW FOR SOME REALLY YUCKY BITS!

This is the real Castle Dracula, which means "son of the dragon," in what used to be Transylvania (now it's part of Romania).

Monster Breath

Eat garlic. It not only keeps away vampires (and everyone else), but also kisses goodbye to bacteria.

Blood Monsters

Dracula, the bloodthirstiest monster of them all, was make-believe. But behind him lurks the shadow of a very real monster—Prince Vlad the Impaler. Vlad Dracula was a 15th century prince, intent on ridding Transylvania of its Turkish rulers. He impaled hundreds of Turks on wooden stakes and watched his victims squirm to their deaths. Vlad Dracula had a thing about stakes. How appropriate that the vampire Dracula meets his end with a stake through the heart.

The belief in blood-sucking vampires was probably based on two diseases. The first is tuberculosis: it used to be called consumption, because people who suffered from it seemed to waste away or be eaten up. Tuberculosis is highly infectious, and spreads quickly in crowded living conditions. This might have led to the idea that members of a vampire's family were the vampire's first meal. People believed that family members were doomed because the first person in the family to die returned as a vampire to make a meal of relatives.

The second disease that looks like vampirism is porphyria. Porphyria is a rare blood disease. People who suffer from it can't stand sunlight. They don't burst into flame at the first rays of the sun, but it can be very painful for them. Porphyria can also make them glow in the dark, which would look pretty eerie. The treatment for this illness? A dose of—you guessed it—blood!

Prescription: Take Three Leeches a Day

A long time ago, doctors used leeches to bleed patients who had all kinds of complaints. (Wouldn't you complain if someone stuck a leech on you?) Now, doctors use leeches to treat patients who have fingers, ears or toes sewn back on after accidents. When doctors need to re-attach, say, a finger, the surgeon can sew the tough arteries together, but veins are too flimsy. Until new veins grow, blood flows into the re-attached finger but very little flows out. And that's bad. Three leeches a day on the finger reduces swelling and keeps it healthy while it heals. And leech bites (which don't hurt) bleed for 12 hours after the leeches drop off, keeping the pressure down in the finger until the next feeding time.

Leech Facts

- In 20 minutes a leech can suck 10 times its own body mass in blood and bloat up to the size of half a fat cigar.
- Never drop a blood-bloated leech into a jar full of unfed leeches. The hungry leeches will smell blood and attack.
- A leech has three sharp-toothed jaws that leave a Y-shaped wound looking just like the Mercedes-Benz logo.